SQUARE BEAK

SQUARE BEAK

CHYNG FENG SUN

ILLUSTRATED BY
CHIHSIEN CHEN

HOUGHTON MIFFLIN COMPANY

BOSTON 1993

Acknowledgments

I want to thank my editor, Audrey Bryant, who is my Bor-luh. (Another book is needed to explain the classic Chinese story of how Bor-luh recognized the one-thousand-mile horse.) Even though I've never been tested on how fast I can run, Audrey treats me like a real one.

I want to thank my friends: Dawn Carrelli, Denise Gilardi, Cathy Anderson, Heidi Werntz, Anita Hum, Ed McInnis, Emily Woolf, Robert Major and Ken Farrell for their help in English writing; Wen-Ya Kuei; and Miguel Picker who makes me laugh and, very often, groan.

Ms. Shaw-Lan Wang's special support is deeply appreciated.

Library of Congress Cataloging-in-Publication Data

Sun, Chyng Feng.
   Square Beak / Chyng Feng Sun ; illustrated by Chihsien Chen.
      p.   cm.
   Summary: Square Beak, famous for the beautiful and unusual eggs
she lays, abandons an egg-laying contest the other chickens expect
her to win and returns to the life she loves, traveling and
dreaming.
   ISBN 0-395-64567-0
   [1. Chickens — Fiction.   2. Eggs — Fiction.   3. Contests — Fiction.
4. Individuality — Fiction.]   I. Chen, Chihsien, ill.   II. Title.
PZ7.S9565Sq   1993   92-19093
[E] — dc20   CIP
                            AC

Printed in the United States of America

WOZ   10   9   8   7   6   5   4   3   2   1

獻給親愛的爸爸，媽媽

To my dear mother and father—C.F.S.

To my mother—C.C.

A beam of soft moonlight poured through the window of a dark henhouse. Several chickens surrounded an old hen, Lao Lao, and her first egg, whispering nervously.

"Did you see what I just saw?"

"What did you see?"

"I asked you first."

"If you don't tell me what you saw, how could I know if we saw the same thing?"

Lao Lao was puzzled and asked if there was anything wrong with her egg.

"Oh, no, it is just so . . . so unique."

"Absolutely special."

"I have never seen an egg quite like it."

Lao Lao took the comments as compliments. "Tomorrow morning, I'll take a really good look at it," she said with an exhausted smile, "and I'll see if you are just being nice."

The next morning, as soon as Lao Lao woke up, she thought of her dear baby. She pulled the egg close and kissed it. Suddenly she froze, blinked her eyes, and finally cried, "Why, it's . . . it's square!"

The same chickens who had congratulated her the night before rushed in to comfort her.

"You should throw it away," a rooster suggested. "There's probably a demon inside of it."

"No," Lao Lao said firmly. "It's my baby. It may be different, but it will never be evil."

After several weeks of waiting for her egg to hatch, Lao Lao was awakened early one morning by a tiny squeaky sound. "Mommy, let me out of here!"

Lao Lao started pecking the egg at once. Finally, a chick, all wet, tumbled out. Lao Lao held her tightly and felt relieved that the chick looked normal except for a square beak. "No wonder she couldn't break the shell," Lao Lao said to herself.

The other chickens named the newborn chick Square Beak.

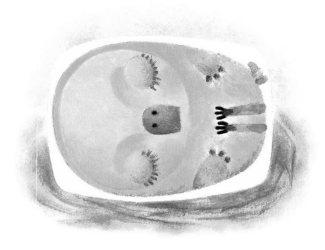

Square Beak was very small, mainly because she didn't get enough to eat—her square beak wasn't good for pecking, so she couldn't compete with the others for food. She felt lonely. The other chicks all liked to play pecking pebbles games, but when Square Beak tried to play, no one wanted her on their team. She usually ended up walking away, and would go see her mother. Lao Lao would give Square Beak some food she had saved and encourage her to play with others. Square Beak would go out, but always to find a comfortable corner to play alone in.

One day, Square Beak noticed a hole in the fence. She stared at it for a while, then crawled out through it. She followed a dirt road that led her down to a winding brook. On the bank, Square Beak found flowers and berries that sparkled like jewels in the tall green grass. She timidly tasted them and the exotic flavors delighted her. She ate more. Finally she lay down in the grass, watching grasshoppers jumping merrily around.

That night, Square Beak slept soundly in her coop and dreamed. In her dream, she returned to the riverside, strolling along the bank, tasting again the flowers and berries. When she woke up, she was surprised to find a tiny pink egg. She nuzzled her first egg, then carefully covered it with hay.

Later that morning, Square Beak went through the broken fence without hesitation, looking for more adventure. This time she found an orange grove. She walked around, looking here and there, eating the fallen oranges. That night she had a dream of a tree growing suns. When each fruit was ripe, it fell from the tree, waiting until the next morning to replace the sun in the sky. When she awoke, she found an egg, round and golden yellow. Every day, Square Beak journeyed to a different place. Every night, she dreamed and laid a special egg. She didn't tell anyone about this except her mother.

One morning a rooster woke up Square Beak. "Come with me!" he said. "We can't find anyone else for the pecking pebbles game."

Square Beak stood up. "What's that?" the rooster asked, pointing at a blue egg with white patches.

Square Beak remembered her dream of a summer sky and said, "That's my egg." At the rooster's unbelieving expression, she moved the hay to show her other eggs. The surprised rooster ran from the henhouse shouting, "Come see Square Beak's eggs!"

Square Beak suddenly became very popular. All day long, chickens surrounded her, wanting to hear her traveling tales and dreams. Some faraway chicken houses even invited her to visit. Square Beak had no time for herself, not even for dreaming.

"Are you happy?" Square Beak asked her mother. "They all like me now."

"I am happy if you are truly happy," Lao Lao replied. "Are you?" But Square Beak was too busy to think.

Soon it was time for the yearly Egg Contest. According to the rules, the participants had to remain in their own coops for four whole days. On the fifth morning, the judges would choose a winner from each hen's best egg. All the chickens chose Square Beak to represent them, and Rooster the Big elected himself to take care of Square Beak during the contest. He said that he knew the secret to laying beautiful eggs.

When they arrived at the farm where the contest was to take place, Rooster the Big told her, "If you lay an egg every morning, then we'll have . . ." he counted his toes, "five eggs from which to choose for the judges." He brought Square Beak six meals a day and insisted she exercise and exercise. The first two nights Square Beak went to sleep with her mind blank and her body aching. And to the surprise of both, Square Beak didn't lay a single egg.

On the third morning, Rooster the Big stormed out of the henhouse and didn't come back for a whole day and night.

In her hunger and loneliness, Square Beak dreamed of her mother, who asked her, "Are you happy?"

Square Beak awakened early the next morning. In the dim light she saw a small, plain white egg. She hugged it tightly. Looking around her tiny, stifling room for a while, she finally got up and covered the egg with straw. Square Beak stood in the doorway, thinking of the contest rules and the chickens who expected her to win. She walked out.

The syrupy aroma of overripe fruit led her to a hilltop full of mango trees. After eating several mangos, Square Beak leaned on a tree and watched the sun rise. As she breathed in the cool morning air, Square Beak reexperienced the joy she had felt when traveling, dreaming, and laying eggs. She also remembered those busy but empty days after her special talents had been discovered.

Square Beak stayed on the hill for a whole day. That night, she closed her eyes under the gentle and comforting moon. For the first time she saw herself in a dream.

A loud noise from below awakened Square Beak.
"Lily is the winner!" the chickens shouted.

"So the contest is over," Square Beak thought. She
felt relieved, but a little disappointed too. Then she
cheered up. "I am going home and I'll see Mother." She
stood up and saw her egg . . .

Suddenly Square Beak was shocked to see a whole
flock of chickens running toward her. "She's here!"
they yelled.

Rooster the Big pushed the other chickens aside and
made his way to Square Beak. "Running away?" he
shouted. "How could you be so irresponsible?"

"Irresponsible?" Square Beak looked him straight in
the eye until he shuffled his feet and lowered his head—
then froze when he saw Square Beak's egg. He picked it
up and held it high above his head. "Let the judges see
this," he crowed. "They'll change their minds and give
us first prize!"

Several chickens rushed off to call the judges. The judges came and examined the egg, then talked together in low voices. Finally, the head judge announced that a final decision had been made. "First prize! First prize!" many chickens shouted, anticipating victory. "According to the rules," the head judge said, "the winning egg must be laid inside the winner's coop to prevent any cheating. A rule is a rule." The crowd stirred. She continued, "Even though Square Beak can't win any prize, we officially declare that this is the most beautiful egg we have ever seen."

Returning from the contest, Square Beak went back to her old life. She traveled, dreamed, and laid eggs. Some eggs were beautiful. Some were strange, or even ugly. She treasured them all. One evening when Square Beak came back from a journey, she was stopped by several young chicks. "Aren't you bored all alone?" they asked. "And wild food tastes awful. Why are you so different?"

Square Beak thought of the rock cave she had discovered that afternoon and wondered what dream she might have that night. Finally she smiled and replied in a quiet voice, "Because I enjoy it."